P9-DDD-955

GATEWAY TO IMAGINATION®

A Book Club from Discovery Toys

Open a book and unlock your
gateway to imagination

From the Library of

MAXWELL HAND

Item#9620601   3/92

Is Your Mama A Llama?

Is Your Mama

by DEBORAH GUARIN

a Llama?

pictures by STEVEN KELLOGG

SCHOLASTIC INC. / New York

Text copyright © 1989 by Deborah Guarino.
Illustrations copyright © 1989 by Steven Kellogg.
Design by Theresa Fitzgerald.
All rights reserved. Published by Scholastic Inc.
SCHOLASTIC HARDCOVER is a registered trademark
of Scholastic Inc.

No part of this publication may be reproduced in whole or in part, or stored
in a retrieval system, or transmitted in any form or by any means, electronic,
mechanical, photocopying, recording, or otherwise, without written permission
of the publisher. For information regarding permission, write to Scholastic Inc.,
730 Broadway, New York, NY 10003.

Library of Congress Cataloging-in-Publication Data

Guarino, Deborah,
    Is your mama a llama?

Summary: A young llama asks his friends if their mamas are llamas
and finds out, in rhyme, that their mothers are other types of animals.
[1. Llamas—Fiction. 2. Animals—Fiction, 3. Stories in rhyme]
I. Kellogg, Steven, ill. II. Title.
PZ8.3.G941s 1989   [E]   87-32315
ISBN 0-590-41387-2

12 11 10 9 8 7 6   1 2 3 4/9

Printed in the U.S.A.   36
First Scholastic printing, September 1989

For my son, Joshua,
My Papa and Mama,
My friends Star and Luci . . .
And that one special llama!
                    — *D.G.*

Love to
Tatia,
Tremaine,
and to their
marvelous mama.
      — *Steven Kellogg*

"Is your mama a llama?" I asked my friend Dave.

"No, she is not," is the answer Dave gave.

"She hangs by her feet, and she lives in a cave.
I do not believe that's how llamas behave."

"Oh," I said. "You are right about that.
   I think that your mama sounds more like a . . .

"Is your mama a llama?" I asked my friend Fred.

"No, she is not," is what Freddy said.

"She has a long neck and white feathers and wings.
I don't think a llama has all of those things."

"Oh," I said. "You don't need to go on.
I think that your mama must be a . . .

"Swan!"

"Is your mama a llama?" I asked my friend Jane.

"No, she is not," Jane politely explained.

"She grazes on grass, and she likes to say, 'Moo!'
I don't think that is what a llama would do."

"Oh," I said. "I understand, now.
I think that your mama must be a . . .

"No, she is not," is how Clyde replied.

"She's got flippers and whiskers and eats fish all day . . .
I do not think llamas act quite in that way."

"Oh," I said. "I'm beginning to feel
  that your mama must really be a . . .

"Seal!"

"Is your mama a llama?" I asked my friend Rhonda.

"No, she is not," is how Rhonda responded.

"She's got big hind legs and a pocket for me . . .
So I don't think a llama is what she could be."

"Oh," I said. "That is certainly true.
I think that your mama's a . . .

"Kangaroo!"

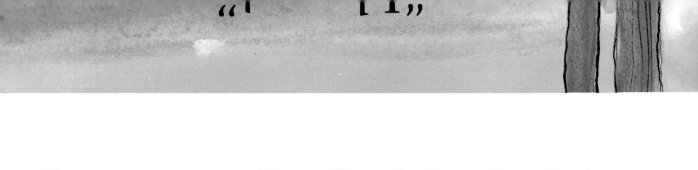

"Is your mama a llama?" I asked my friend Llyn.

"Oh, Lloyd, don't be silly!" Llyn said with a grin.

"My mama has big ears, long lashes, and fur . . .
And you, of all people, should know about her!"

"Our mamas belong to the same herd, and *you*,
know all about llamas, 'cause you are one, too!"

"Yes, you are right," I said to my friend.
"*My* mama's a . . .

THE END